Poppy and Max and the Fashion Show

Sally Grindley ❧ Lindsey Gardiner

ORCHARD BOOKS

Poppy and Max and the Fashion Show

For Daphne
SG

For Dean, a boy who likes his fashion! xx
LG

Reading Consultant: Prue Goodwin,
lecturer in education at the University of Reading

ORCHARD BOOKS
338 Euston Road, London NW1 3BH
Orchard Books Australia
Level 17/207 Kent Street, Sydney, NSW 2000
ISBN 978 1 84362 399 1 (hardback)
ISBN 978 1 84362 393 9 (paperback)
First published in hardback in 2007 by Orchard Books
First paperback publication in 2008
Poppy and Max characters © Lindsey Gardiner 2001
Text © Sally Grindley 2007
Illustrations © Lindsey Gardiner 2007
The rights of Sally Grindley to be identified as the author and
of Lindsey Gardiner to be identified as the illustrator of this work
have been asserted by them in accordance with the
Copyright, Designs and Patents Act, 1988.
A CIP catalogue record for this book is available from the British Library.

1 3 5 7 9 10 8 6 4 2 (hardback)
1 3 5 7 9 10 8 6 4 2 (paperback)
Printed in China

Orchard Books is a division of Hachette Children's Books

www.orchardbooks.co.uk

One day, Poppy and Max were
out walking when they saw a poster
outside the village hall.

The poster reads:

MODELS
WANTED
FOR
FASHION SHOW
PLEASE
COME INSIDE!

"Brilliant!" cried Poppy. "I love
dressing up."
"I am not a dog who likes wearing
clothes," sniffed Max.

"Please come in with me," said Poppy.
"As long as I don't have to dress up
too," said Max.
The hall was crowded with people.
Poppy spotted some of her friends.

"Hello Chloe," she called. "Hello Jack, hello Sam."

"Hello Poppy and Max," they said.

"Come and try on some clothes."

"Brilliant!" said Poppy. "I'm going
to try on this ballgown."

EVENING WEAR

"Why don't you put on this catsuit, Max?" laughed Jack.
"Very funny," growled Max.

"Look at these boots, Max," giggled Chloe. "You could be Dog-in-Boots."
"I don't want to be dog-in-anything," said Max huffily.

Max tried to walk round the hall.

Someone trod on his foot.

"Ow!" he squealed. "Let me out of here."

Someone elbowed him in the face.
"Ouch!" he howled. "I want to
go home."

He jumped up on to a high platform
to get out of the way.

"What's that dog doing on the catwalk?" someone shouted. The hall went very quiet and everyone looked at Max.

"Come down, Max," called Poppy.
Max was about to jump down when
a voice cried, "What a handsome dog!"
Max put up an ear.

"That dog could be our star performer,"
the voice continued.

Max stuck his nose in the air and tried
to look important.

"But Max is not a dog who likes
wearing clothes," Poppy said to
the director of the show.

"I can change my mind," sniffed Max. "What would you like me to wear?"

"Come with me," said the director. "Everyone else get ready. We're about to begin."

Someone put on some music.

Someone turned on a spotlight.

Everyone lined up at the end
of the catwalk.
The show began.

Poppy modelled
a cowgirl outfit
and boots.

Jack modelled
a pair of shorts
and a hoodie.

Chloe modelled
a nightdress and
carried a bear.

And then it was Max's turn.
He poked his head out from
behind a curtain.

"Come on, Max. Don't be shy,"
cried Poppy.
"His ears have gone all curly,"
said Jack.
"He looks scared," said Chloe.

Someone pushed Max
out on to the catwalk.

He was wearing . . . a white poodle
suit, with a pink bow round his ear.

Poppy clapped her hands. "Brilliant!"
she cried.
"Max is having a bad fur day,"
Jack cried.

Max trotted down the catwalk as fast
as the poodle suit would let him.

When he reached the end, he leapt
to the floor and ran out of the hall.

Poppy found him outside hiding
behind a bush.

"What's the matter, Max?" she asked.

"I am not a dog who likes wearing
clothes," mumbled Max. "And now
I am stuck in this silly poodle suit."

"You look very sweet," said Poppy.
"But you don't look like my Max."
She helped him out of the suit.

Max fluffed up his ears
and shook out his fur.
"I'll never dress up again,"
he said.

"A handsome dog like you
doesn't need to," smiled Poppy.

Max stuck his nose in the air.
"Quite right," he said. "A handsome
dog like me doesn't need to."

Sally Grindley
Illustrated by Lindsey Gardiner

Poppy and Max and the Lost Puppy   978 1 84362 394 6 £4.99

Poppy and Max and the Snow Dog   978 1 84362 404 2 £4.99

Poppy and Max and the Fashion Show   978 1 84362 393 9 £4.99

Poppy and Max and the Sore Paw   978 1 84362 405 9 £4.99

Poppy and Max and the River Picnic   978 1 84362 395 3 £4.99

Poppy and Max and the Noisy Night   978 1 84362 409 7 £4.99

Poppy and Max and the Big Wave   978 1 84362 519 3 £4.99

Poppy and Max and Too Many Muffins 978 1 84362 410 3 £4.99

Poppy and Max are available from all good bookshops,
or can be ordered direct from the publisher:
Orchard Books, PO BOX 29, Douglas IM99 1BQ
Credit card orders please telephone 01624 836000 or fax 01624 837033
or e-mail: bookshop@enterprise.net for details.

To order please quote title, author and ISBN and your full name and address.
Cheques and postal orders should be made payable to 'Bookpost plc'.
Postage and packing is FREE within the UK
(overseas customers should add £1.00 per book).

Prices and availability are subject to change.